TERROR IN THE CITY

The 1906 San Francisco Earthquake

Bonnie Highsmith Taylor

COVER-TO-COVER BOOKS

Chapter 2

Perfection Learning®

FAIR OAKS

Illustrations: Dea Marks

About the Author

Bonnie Highsmith Taylor is a native Oregonian. She loves camping in the Oregon mountains and watching birds and other wildlife. Writing is Ms. Taylor's first love. But she also enjoys going to plays and concerts, collecting antique dolls, and listening to good music.

Ms. Taylor is the author of several Animal Adventures books, including *Lucy: A Virginia Opossum* and *Zelda: A Little Brown Bat*. She has also written novels, including *Gypsy in the Cellar* and *Kodi's Mare*.

Image Credits: ArtToday (www.arttoday.com) p. 13; Dover Publications p. 9; Library of Congress cover, pp. 3 (bottom), 16 (top), 33, 54, 56; National Archives pp. 16 (bottom), 18, 25, 31, 46, 49 (middle); NOAA pp. 22, 26, 29, 49 (top), 49 (bottom)

For information, contact
Perfection Learning® Corporation
1000 North Second Avenue, P.O. Box 500
Logan, Iowa 51546-0500
Phone: 1-800-831-4190 • Fax: 1-712-644-2392
perfectionlearning.com

Paperback ISBN 0-7891-5619-9
Cover Craft® ISBN 0-7569-0456-0
2 3 4 5 6 7 PP 08 07 06 05 04 03

TABLE OF CONTENTS

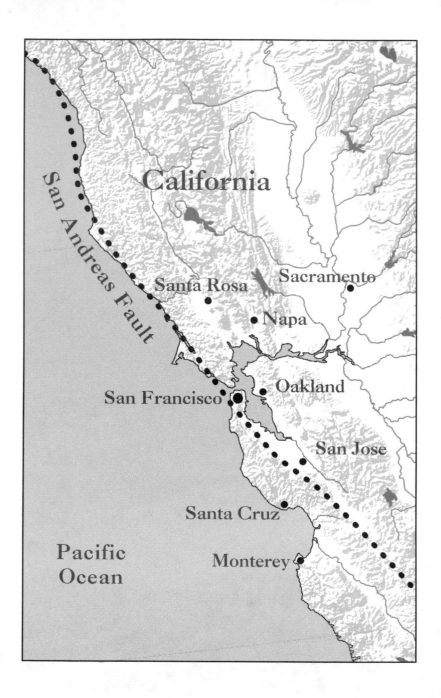

California

San Andreas Fault

Santa Rosa

Sacramento

Napa

San Francisco

Oakland

San Jose

Santa Cruz

Pacific
Ocean

Monterey

Chapter 1

"Stuart," Papa whispered. "It's time to get up."

Stuart groaned. He turned over. Then he pulled a blanket over his head.

Papa shook Stuart softly. He pulled off Stuart's blanket.

"Stuart, get up," Papa said. "It's after four o'clock."

Stuart blinked and rubbed his eyes. He was so sleepy. And the room was so dark.

Then Stuart remembered. Today was the day! He was going on Papa's milk route.

Stuart sat up in bed.

"Sh-h-h," Papa whispered. "Don't wake your sister."

Stuart had a three-year-old sister, Betsy. She was asleep in a crib in the corner.

Stuart slipped out of bed. In no time, he was dressed. He was excited about going with Papa.

Mr. Ross delivered milk and butter in downtown San Francisco. He supplied the big hotels and restaurants.

Ten-year-old Stuart had always wanted to go with Papa. And Papa said he was now old enough.

It was Wednesday, April 18, 1906. School was closed for Easter vacation.

Stuart went into the kitchen. Mama dished up a big bowl of oatmeal. She buttered a thick slice of bread.

"Hurry and eat," she said. "Papa is almost ready."

Papa was hitching Dolly to the milk wagon. Dolly had been pulling the wagon as long as Stuart could remember. She knew every stop on the route. Papa didn't have to guide her at all.

"I don't know what I would do without old Dolly," Papa had always said. "But she is getting old. Someday soon, I will have to break in a new horse."

Stuart was so excited. He could hardly eat. Mama kept saying, "Eat your oatmeal before it gets cold."

Finally, Stuart swallowed the last bite. He put on his hat.

"Stay with Papa," Mama said. "I don't want you lost in that awful city."

Stuart smiled.

Mrs. Ross always called San Francisco "that awful city." She said a lot of bad things went on there.

Mr. Ross agreed. But he said, "There are good people and bad people everywhere."

Mr. Ross had been born in San Francisco. His father had helped build some of the buildings there.

Mrs. Ross had come from a farm in Ohio. She didn't like cities. She never went into the city unless she had to. She had Mr. Ross do most of the shopping.

Stuart had only seen San Francisco once. And that was four years ago. He had had a bad toothache. Papa took him to a dentist to have his tooth pulled. Stuart hardly remembered the city.

But today he was going there. He would see all the places Papa had told him about. The fine hotels and the city hall. The Grand Opera House and the newspaper office buildings. He might even visit Chinatown.

Papa had told him about the Chinese people. They had come to California long ago. They dressed as they had in China Papa told Stuart. Men and women both wore long trousers and long blouses called *tunics*. The men had long braids called *queues*.

Before gold was discovered in California, fewer than 20 Chinese lived in the United States. By 1850, there were about 45. Three years later, about 15,000 lived in the U.S.

Many more Chinese **immigrants** came when the railroads were being built. They worked for less money than white men. And they were more **reliable**.

By 1870, about 100,000 Chinese people lived west of the Sierra Nevada. Thirty thousand made their homes in one section of San Francisco. It became known as Chinatown.

Stuart thought it sounded very interesting. He hoped he would be able to see Chinatown.

Chapter 2

Stuart climbed up to the high wagon seat. He felt proud sitting next to Papa.

It was still dark. The early morning air felt good to Stuart.

Papa clicked his tongue at Dolly. She knew that meant it was time to go.

The milk bottles and cans rattled in back. The only other sound was Dolly's *clop-clop*.

As the day grew lighter, Stuart could hear birds singing. Then a rooster crowed.

After a while, Stuart saw lights off in the distance.

"Is that the city, Papa?" he asked.

"Yes," Mr. Ross answered. "That's San Francisco."

Stuart felt a shiver go through him. San Francisco! He was going to San Francisco!

"What's that noise?" asked Stuart.

"It's dogs barking," Papa answered.

"It sounds like a whole lot of dogs," Stuart said.

"Yes, it does at that," said Papa. "Wonder what's gotten into them."

Suddenly, Dolly lurched. She whinnied. Then she stopped dead still.

Papa clicked his tongue. "Get up there, Dolly."

The horse moved a few feet. Then she lurched again.

"What's wrong with you, old girl?" asked Mr. Ross.

Dolly shook her head and snorted. Then she trotted on.

"Can't imagine what's gotten into her," said Mr. Ross.

The barking had nearly stopped.

The wagon entered the city. Dolly pulled the wagon down a familiar street.

After a few moments, Papa pointed at a building. "Look, Stuart," he said. "There's the Grand Opera House."

The Grand Opera House was built between 1873 and 1876 by Dr. Thomas Wade. The opera house opened the night of January 17, 1876. The first performance was called *Snowflake*.

The evening of April 17, 1906, the famous **tenor**, Enrico Caruso, performed in the opera *Carmen*. Three thousand people attended.

The opera house burned to the ground in one of the fires resulting from the earthquake. The site is now a parking lot.

13

Stuart stared at the building. He had heard Papa talk about the building so often.

Papa said, "Last night Caruso sang there. He sang in the opera *Carmen*."

"Who is he?" Stuart asked.

"Enrico Caruso is the most popular opera singer in the world," Papa sighed. "How your mama would love to hear him sing."

Stuart looked again at the building. "Someday," Stuart said to himself. "Someday, I will take Mama to the Grand Opera House. She will hear this Caruso sing."

A little farther down the street, Dolly stopped in front of a building.

"Good girl," Papa said. "This is the Palace Hotel. This is where Caruso is staying."

Papa climbed down from the wagon. Stuart took the reins. "I'll hold Dolly," he said.

Papa laughed. "Dolly doesn't need to be held. She's made these same stops hundreds of times. She could do the route all by herself."

Mr. Ross lifted a large milk can from the wagon. He carried it inside the building. Then he came back. He took three packages of butter from the wagon and carried them into the building.

Stuart sat on the wagon seat. He looked all around. He never dreamed buildings could be so huge.

Other wagons were moving along the streets. A man driving a bakery wagon waved at Stuart. Stuart waved back.

Another wagon stopped in front of a building down the street. Two men came out. They were carrying big stacks of newspapers. They put them in the wagon.

The *San Francisco Call* was a newspaper. In early years it shared a building with the United States Mint. This branch of the mint made currency, or money, for public use. Today, the San Francisco mint only makes proof sets and commemorative coins.

At one time, Mark Twain worked for the newspaper.

Construction of the 22-story Call Building was started in September 1895. It was completed on December 17, 1897.

The Call Building was supposed to be earthquake-proof and fireproof. The building suffered little damage from the earthquake. But the interior was nearly destroyed in the 1906 fire. The temperature of the burning building was estimated at 2000°F.

After the building was renovated in the 1930s, it was called Central Towers.

Papa came back. He got in the wagon. Dolly clopped along. She stopped at the building where the men had loaded the newspapers.

"This is the Call Building," Papa told Stuart. "This is where one of San Francisco's newspapers is printed."

Stuart looked puzzled. "You deliver milk to a newspaper office?" he asked.

Mr. Ross laughed. "Some of the men who work here are friends. They buy cream from me for their coffee."

Papa took a pint of cream into the office. When he came back, a man was with him.

"Stuart," Mr. Ross said. "This is Mr. Cohen. He is a photographer. He works for the *Call*."

Mr. Cohen shook Stuart's hand. "Pleased to meet you, young fellow," he said. "Your father has told me what a fine boy you are."

Stuart beamed. Mr. Cohen went back into the building.

Nob Hill stands 338 feet above the city. In the mid-1850s, the first house was built on the hill. It was built where the elegant Fairmont Hotel now stands.

The Fairmont Hotel was first built in the early 1900s. It was completed on the eve of the 1906 earthquake. Two days later, it was destroyed by fire. In 1907, the hotel was rebuilt.

In the 1870s, several railroad tycoons and other rich people built mansions on the hill. Most of these mansions were destroyed in the 1906 fire.

The name Nob Hill is said to come from the word *Nabob*, which means "a rich and important person."

Mr. Ross pointed north. "Up there is Nob Hill," he said.

Stuart gasped. Papa had told him about the rich people who lived on Nob Hill. "Some of the richest people in the world," he had said.

Stuart gazed at the buildings in the distance.

What would it be like to live in a house with over 50 rooms? Stuart wondered. Papa had said they were like castles.

Once more, Dolly began to act strangely. She **nickered** loudly.

"There, there, old girl," Papa said. "It's all right now."

Another wagon came down the street toward them. The horse pulling that wagon was also acting up. It took several seconds for the driver to calm the horse.

"I can't understand it," Papa murmured.

Dolly settled down. Slowly, the wagon moved along Market Street.

Stuart turned back and forth on the wagon seat. There were so many sights to see. What an exciting place San Francisco was!

Many scientists believe that some animals can sense an earthquake before it happens. Dogs often howl. Horses become nervous. Flocks of seagulls often fly away from the shore. Rats have been seen running along power lines before an earthquake.

In one case, just before an earthquake, a herd of cows stampeded and broke down fences.

Chapter 3

Dolly moved very slowly. Mr. Ross tried to hurry her.

Stuart was surprised at how noisy the city was. And it was only a little after five o'clock.

Suddenly, Stuart heard a different noise. It was a deep, rumbling roar.

The roar got louder. It was deafening.

What is *that*? Stuart wondered.

Dolly screamed. Other horses were also screaming.

The roar seemed to come from below the street. Stuart tried to speak. His voice froze in his throat.

Stuart saw the terror in Papa's eyes. The ground began to move. The milk wagon rocked to one side.

Mingled with the roaring were human screams. Some of the screams came from the Palace Hotel. Glass was falling from the broken windows. The Call Building was swaying back and forth.

"Papa! Papa!" Stuart yelled.

"Earthquake!" cried Papa. "Jump, Stuart!"

If one or two bricks near the bottom of a brick wall slip out of place, the wall will weaken. Eventually, the wall will crumble.

Beneath the ground are layers of rocks, like the bricks in a wall. Sometimes these layers start to sag. Large rocks may slip out of place. This causes the upper layers to shift and crack. A crack is called a *fault*, or a shift.

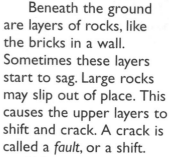

When rocks along the fault move, they cause the earth to shake—like a bowl of gelatin. Sometimes the movement is so strong the earth splits on the surface.

Some faults are many miles long. The San Andreas Fault follows the California coastline. It runs from the northwest part of the state to the Gulf of California. It passes within eight miles of the center of San Francisco.

Faults are found in many places in the world. Some have caused strong earthquakes. Powerful earthquakes have been recorded in China, India, Bolivia, and Mexico.

There have been numerous earthquakes in San Francisco. But the 1906 earthquake is believed to have been the strongest ever recorded. It measured 8.5 on the **Richter Scale**.

Another San Francisco earthquake happened in 1989 during a World Series baseball game. Freeways collapsed. Many people were killed.

That earthquake registered 7.1 on the Richter Scale and lasted only 15 seconds.

But before they could jump, Stuart and Mr. Ross were thrown from the wagon. They hit the ground hard.

A split second later, a pile of bricks completely covered the wagon. Dolly's pitiful cries echoed in Stuart's ears. Then she lay still beneath the rubble.

Some of the bricks landed on Papa. A gash opened on his forehead. Blood spurted.

"Oh, Papa!" Stuart cried. "You're bleeding!"

Mr. Ross took a handkerchief from his jacket pocket. He held it on the wound. "It's all right, Stuart," he said. "It's only a scratch. Are *you* hurt?"

"No—no, Papa," answered Stuart. "I'm—I'm fine."

Stuart was not hurt. But he was shaking so hard he couldn't get up.

Mr. Ross tried to get to his feet. But one leg crumpled beneath him.

"Oh, no," he groaned. "My ankle. I think it's broken."

Stuart got up. His legs were wobbly, and his head pounded.

All around, Stuart heard screaming and moaning. He had never been so frightened in his life.

"Can—can you walk, Papa?" he asked in a whisper.

Mr. Ross hopped a few steps. He held on to Stuart's shoulder. "A little," he answered. "Maybe it's only sprained."

Stuart looked down. His father's ankle was bruised and badly swollen.

The ground was still trembling. Stones and bricks were falling. In every direction, church bells were clanging.

Stuart looked all around. Trolley tracks were twisted. Wires were down everywhere.

Not far away, the street had opened up. Water was spurting into the air.

The tall buildings swayed from side to side. Then the top of one tumbled to the ground. The sound made Stuart jump. He felt his father's hand tighten on his shoulder.

Stuart suddenly thought of home. He thought of Mama and little Betsy.

Are they all right? Stuart wondered. Is their house still standing?

Stuart looked up at Papa. He knew Papa was thinking the same thing.

All around, more church bells clanged. The roaring went on and on. It was like a continuous roll of thunder. Then, 45 seconds after it started, it stopped.

But the screams continued. The awful sound made Stuart feel like crying.

Roaring is caused by the vibration of rocks below the earth crashing together. It's like the way the ground vibrates when a freight train rumbles by.

"Papa," Stuart murmured. "Dolly's dead."

Papa hugged Stuart. "I know, son. I know. She was a good and faithful horse."

Ten seconds after the big roar ended, a second **tremor** began. Again the earth rocked furiously. Buildings crumbled.

The second tremor seemed worse than the first. Mr. Ross staggered and fell. More streets split open. Water and gas shot into the air.

The screaming didn't stop. People ran around in circles.

"Mary! Mary!" a man was crying. "Where are you?"

Beneath city streets are pipes that carry water and gas. Earthquakes often cause these pipes to break.

A baby was crying. Horses ran through the streets neighing loudly. Many pulled empty wagons.

Stuart fought back tears. He helped his father to his feet. But the rolling earth sent them both to the ground.

The smell of gas in the air made Stuart's stomach churn. Then he heard the cry of "Fire! Fire!"

Chapter 4

Flames shot up from several buildings. The air filled with smoke.

Once more, Stuart and Mr. Ross got to their feet. People were running in all directions. Many of them were only half-dressed.

Someone was screaming, "There's no water! The city's on fire. And there's no water!"

A man with a camera stopped across the street from Stuart and Mr. Ross. It was Mr. Cohen. He was the man from the newspaper. He took several pictures of the damage. Then he moved on down Market Street.

An old man grabbed Mr. Ross's arm. "Have you seen Anna? Please help me find Anna."

Papa patted the old man's arm as he passed. Papa hopped along holding Stuart's shoulder.

Stuart saw tears in Papa's eyes. He had never seen Papa cry before. Stuart wiped tears from his own eyes.

Still more fires were breaking out.

Within 17 minutes after the first quake, nearly 50 fires were burning. The earthquake and fires caused an estimated $400 million in damage. Fires were responsible for $320 million of that amount.

Stuart and his father moved along slowly. Mr. Ross **winced** with every step.

"Where are we going, Papa?" asked Stuart.

Mr. Ross did not answer. He gasped with pain. Then finally, he said, "Home. We're going home."

But how? Stuart wondered.

How could they go home? It was such a long way. And Dolly was dead. Papa could hardly walk.

They came to a pile of bricks and splintered wood. Four men were throwing the bricks aside. A low moaning sound came from under the rubble.

Stuart saw a woman's arm. He saw long brown hair. The moaning grew weaker.

Stuart picked up a brick. He threw it to one side. He picked up another and another. He worked faster. He and the four men worked as fast as they could.

At last, one man picked up the young woman. He carried her away.

Stuart took a deep breath. She was alive! The woman was alive!

One of the men patted Stuart on the back. "Good work, son," he said. "Thank you."

Stuart felt good knowing he had helped save a life. Papa smiled at him.

The ground quivered again and again. The smoke grew thicker. People coughed and choked.

It is not known for sure how many people were killed in the San Francisco earthquake. Some early reports said 300. Others said 700. Now it is thought the death toll reached 3,000.

Millions of dollars of damage was done. But most of it was due to the fires rather than the earthquake.

Overhead, live wires dangled from poles. A trolley car lay on its side. Dead horses lay in the street. Stuart held back a sob when he thought of Dolly.

Stuart felt a sharp pang in his stomach. He was surprised to realize it was hunger.

How can I think of hunger at a time like this? he wondered. He thought of the bowl of oatmeal Mama had forced him to eat. How he wished he had another now.

Fire wagons were everywhere. The firemen checked hydrants along the street. It was the same with all of them. There was no water. The men tried pumping water from the sewers.

Then the firemen tried beating out the fires. They used hoses, gunny sacks, and even their jackets.

The wind picked up. The fires grew bigger.

Papa and Stuart could hear the firemen yelling, "Everyone stay back! We're going to dynamite!"

"Why are they going to dynamite, Papa?" asked Stuart.

Papa shook his head. "I'm not sure, son," he answered.

Soon the blasting began. All over the city, buildings were blown up. The horrible sound went on and on.

After a while, Stuart and Papa walked on. They met a man selling apples and oranges for five cents each.

Dynamiting was done to make *firebreaks*. These were wide spaces that the fire could not jump. Then the fires would burn themselves out because there was nothing left to provide fuel.

Dynamiting is no longer used to fight fires in cities. It is still used to fight wildfires.

Papa bought an orange. He handed it to Stuart. "Maybe this will help your thirst," he said.

Stuart smiled and thanked him. He peeled the orange and gave half to his father. It *did* taste good.

Chapter 5

"I must rest, Stuart," Papa said.

Nearby was a little grassy spot with a drinking fountain in the center. But there was no water in the fountain. Stuart helped Papa to the ground.

Other people were sitting or lying on the grass. A young woman held a sleeping baby. The baby whimpered softly. The woman stared into space. She seemed unaware of what was going on.

An old man was on his knees. He was saying the Lord's Prayer over and over.

Another man was holding his wife in his arms. He rocked her back and forth as though she were a child.

Stuart sank down next to Papa. Mr. Ross's ankle was badly swollen. Stuart knew it must be very painful. At least the cut on his father's head had stopped bleeding.

Most people were just sitting. No one was talking. Stuart leaned his head against Papa. He was so tired. He had never been so tired.

Papa's eyes were closed. He was breathing deeply. Stuart closed his eyes.

Suddenly, a loud blast brought Stuart to an upright position.

How long have I slept? he wondered. Papa was awake. But he was still lying down.

Stuart discovered that more people had arrived while he slept. A woman was there with a girl about Stuart's age. The girl was clinging tightly to her mother. She was sobbing.

"There, there, Katy," the woman said. "It's all right. Papa will find us."

An old man lay nearby, wearing only long underwear. The underwear was black from smoke and soot. Stuart saw that his hands were red and blistered.

On the old man's chest lay a Bible. Part of the Bible had been burned. The man was snoring loudly.

Another blast sounded. The old man jerked in his sleep and cried out. The girl sobbed harder.

Stuart shuddered. He looked down Market Street. Soldiers were everywhere. They were carrying guns. Some of them were nailing papers on power poles and boards.

One man got up. He walked to where a paper was nailed. When he came back, he said, "It's a **proclamation** from our mayor."

Mr. Ross sat up. "What does it say?" he asked.

"It says anyone caught looting will be killed," the man answered.

"Killed!" Papa exclaimed. "They—they can't kill people!"

The man made a snorting sound. "Can't they? They'll do anything Mayor Eugene Schmitz tells them to do."

"That's right," someone else added. "Schmitz runs this city. He and that lawyer of his—Abe Ruef."

Eugene Schmitz was once an honest, hardworking citizen of San Francisco. He was married and had two daughters. He had never been involved in any scandal.

But Schmitz was just the kind of man attorney Abe Ruef was looking for. Schmitz was someone Ruef could control. With the help of Ruef, Schmitz became mayor of San Francisco.

For the next five years, the two men got rich through **graft** and **corruption**. They stole money from city funds. They allowed illegal businesses to operate by taking a percentage of their income.

Many people knew of the men's dishonesty. But it was not until after the earthquake that they were arrested. They were both sent to jail.

After Schmitz was released, he had the nerve to run for mayor again. It wasn't surprising that he lost the election.

Stuart had never heard of these people. But he could tell that they weren't very well liked.

"Papa," Stuart whispered. "What's looting?"

"Stealing," Papa answered. "Breaking into places and taking things."

Stuart knew that stealing was wrong. But he couldn't believe that people would be killed for stealing.

The blasting went on all day. Every once in a while the earth trembled. Each time, Stuart's heart jumped to his throat.

Questions swam through Stuart's mind. When would it end? Would he and Papa ever get home again? Would there still be a home to go to? Would Mama and Betsy be unharmed?

People still passed by. They carried the few belongings they had saved. A man pushed a wheelbarrow piled with books. A woman pushed a baby carriage. In the carriage was a baby. Stacked around the baby were glass dishes. A man and a woman carried a mattress with blankets stacked on it.

A young man approached them. Over his shoulder was a gunny sack. He stopped in front of Stuart and Mr. Ross.

The young man looked up and down the street. In a low voice, he said, "Anyone want to buy bread?"

Someone asked, "How much?"

"A dollar a loaf," the young man answered.

"A dollar a loaf!" Papa shouted. "Are you out of your mind?"

Papa was really angry. Stuart had never seen Papa angry before.

One person said, "You probably stole that bread anyway."

The young man stammered, "All right. All right. Fifty cents a loaf. But no less."

Papa bought one loaf. He shared it with the woman holding the baby. Two more people bought bread. The man hurried away.

"What a crook!" one man said.

Stuart remembered what Papa had said. There are good people and bad people everywhere.

The bread was hard and stale. But still Stuart thought nothing had ever tasted so good.

Chapter 6

Stuart and Papa slept on the grass all night. Stuart woke up choking. Smoke was all around.

Some soldiers came to where Stuart and his father were. "You folks will have to move on," one of them said. "The fires are getting close. Even Chinatown is on fire."

As far as Stuart could see were fires. There were too many to count.

The young girl with the baby began to cry. "Where can we go? My husband is dead. Our house is gone."

The old man struggled to get to his feet. One of the soldiers helped him up.

"They have a **refugee** camp set up at Golden Gate Park," the soldier said. "They have an emergency hospital." He looked at the old man's hands. "They'll fix your burns."

The soldiers gave directions to the park. Papa leaned on Stuart's shoulder as they moved on. Papa had to stop and rest several times.

Many of the people heading to the

park were Chinese. Stuart couldn't keep from staring.

One Chinese boy was about Stuart's age. Stuart smiled at him. The boy smiled back. Then he hung his head.

Papa had to rest more and more. His ankle was swelling again. Stuart was worried. What if there was no room for them? So many people were heading in the same direction.

Two men ahead of Stuart and Papa pointed at something. Papa tried to cover Stuart's eyes. But he was not quick enough.

Stuart saw a man propped up against a pile of bricks. A sign was pinned to his coat. It read "Shot for Looting."

Stuart felt his stomach turn.

At last, they reached the park. Hundreds of people were there. Some tents had been set up. They were being used as hospitals.

Volunteers cared for the injured and homeless. The American Red Cross was newly organized. They had almost no funds. President Theodore Roosevelt did send a doctor to represent the Red Cross.

Money and supplies came from everywhere. Nearly $245,000 came from Japan. China sent $40,000. And Mexico sent $15,000.

Smaller amounts, some as little as $50, came from Cuba, India, Australia, and other parts of the world. Three millionaires, John D. Rockefeller, William Waldorf Astor, and Andrew Carnegie, each gave $100,000.

The students at a Native American school in Oregon spent one whole night baking. They sent 830 loaves of bread to San Francisco by Wells Fargo. It took two days to get there. A bakery in Utah also sent a shipment of bread. The Merchants' Association in New York sent 14 boxcar loads of canned goods and $60,000 worth of drugs.

Congress voted $2,500,000 for aid for the victims of the earthquake. They also sent several thousand tents, blankets, cots, and mattresses.

The cries and moans were horrible. Injured people were lined up on the grass outside the tents.

Papa dropped to the ground. "I—I can't go any farther, son," he said.

Stuart sat beside him. People's belongings were all over the park. They had been saved from the fires.

Stuart saw steamer trunks. Some had roller skates nailed to the bottoms. There were sewing machines, tubs and buckets filled with dishes, and rocking chairs. Someone had even saved a piano.

By dusk, Stuart and Papa had settled down on the mattress they had been given. A doctor had wrapped Papa's ankle.

"It feels much better," Papa told Stuart.

They had waited in a breadline for nearly an hour. The beans and bread had tasted good to them. They each had been given an apple.

There was little water. And that was being rationed. It tasted bad. Stuart saw green slime floating in the wooden water bucket.

By the next morning, several hundred more people had arrived. Some food supplies had been brought in on a wagon. The tins of corned beef, potatoes, and fruit looked wonderful.

Stuart thought of all the milk and butter that had been lost with Papa's wagon. How he wished for a cup of milk.

While Papa rested, Stuart wandered around the park. Moans came from the hospital tents. But Stuart also heard cries of newborn babies.

Stuart also heard people talking. Someone said the dynamiting had been stopped until further notice. But the fires were still raging.

Every hour or so a baby was born in the park. One, a baby girl, was named April Francisco Jones. She was the seventeenth baby to be born outdoors after the earthquake.

Another baby born in the park was named Golden Gate. At another refugee camp, 23 babies were born in one day. Many more were born in other parts of the city.

There was almost no water anywhere. The doctors couldn't get enough water to **sterilize** their instruments.

Someone said that the shooting of the looters was still going on.

"From what I saw," an older man said, "the soldiers are doing a lot of the looting themselves."

Saturday morning, Stuart and Papa waited in line for breakfast. Papa's ankle was much better. He could walk without help.

Stuart's stomach rumbled as he smelled the cereal and coffee that was being served.

Suddenly, a young boy came running through the park. "The fires are out!" he shouted. "The fires are out!"

People yelled and cheered. They were hugging and kissing. Papa hugged Stuart.

It was exactly 7:15. The San Francisco fire had finally ended. A few minutes later, it began to rain.

———⎼⎼⥿⥿⥿⥿⥿⥿⥿⥿⎼⎼———

Stuart and Papa were leaving the city! Papa had given a man all the money he had. The man owned a horse and wagon. And he was taking Stuart and Papa home.

The man had wanted ten dollars to take them home. But Papa only had three dollars. They had argued for a long time.

"Maybe someone should be told that you are charging these prices," said Papa.

Angrily, the man finally had agreed to take Papa's three dollars.

No one talked on the long drive. Stuart knew what Papa was thinking. What if Mama and Betsy were not there? What if something had happened to them? What if they were—

The wagon made the last turn in the road toward home. Stuart held his breath.

Then, far ahead, Stuart saw two figures. They were running toward the wagon.

"Mama! Betsy!" Stuart cried.

Through his tears, Stuart saw Mama's outstretched arms. He watched Betsy trying to keep up. Then he could hear her happy laughter.

Stuart and Papa jumped from the wagon before it could stop.

In no time, they were all in one another's arms. They were laughing and crying.

The wagon turned and left. Soon it was out of sight.

San Francisco seemed so far away. Stuart knew that he would never forget the horrible tragedy as long as he lived.

But now—now he was home.

EXTRA THE DAILY NEWS **EXTRA**

VOL. 7. NO. 25. FOURTH YEAR. SAN FRANCISCO, WEDNESDAY EVENING, APRIL 18, 1906. INDEPENDENT. 25c MONTH; 1 COPY.

HUNDREDS DEAD!

Fire Follows Earthquake, Laying Downtown Section in Ruins--City Seems Doomed For Lack of Water

776

KNOWN DEAD
AT MECHANICS' PAVILION

Max Fenner, policeman, killed in collapse Essex Hotel.

Niece of Detective Dillon, killed in collapse, 6th and Shipley.

Unidentified woman, killed at 18 7th st.

Two unknown men, brought in autos.

OTHER DEAD

Five killed, 2 injured, in collapse of building at 239 Geary.

Frank Corali, buried, beneath basement floor of burning lodging house 6th and Mission. Heard crying "For God's sake, help me."

Seven firemen killed in collapse of brick power house Valencia and 7th.

John Wheley and son, killed in

At 126 Langton, 4 killed; Billy Sheehan, policeman, rescued 3 people.

Many injured at 117 6th st., Hotel Phillips.

San Francisco was practically demolished and totally paralyzed by the earthquake, which commenced at 5:11 a. m. today and continued with terrific vigor for four minutes.

Great loss of life was caused by the collapse of buildings, and many people met a more cruel death by fire. Flames broke out in all parts of the city.

The monetary loss caused by the earthquake, the fire which followed it and the depreciation in values that will result will amount to hundreds of millions of dollars.

The progress of San Francisco has received a check from which it will probably take many years to recover.

Thousands of men who went to bed wealthy last night awoke this morning practically bankrupt.

The fury of the temblor was greater than any that has been known in the history of the city.

The people are appalled, terror-stricken. Thousands, fearful of a recurrence of the dreadful disaster, with results still more dire, are hastening out of San Francisco.

Many heart-rending scenes have been enacted. Families are moving their belongings helter-skelter, and moving aimlessly about, keeping in the open.

The City Hall is a complete wreck. The walls surrounding the grand dome have fallen, leaving only the skeleton frame work and the top of the dome intact. Around all sides of the building the walls have crumbled, like so many cards. The Receiving Hospital was buried.

The surgeons moved to Mechanics' Pavilion, which today is a combined hospital and morgue. Dead and dying are brought in by autos, ambulances and even garbage carts.

Francisco Bay.

A building collapsed at Steiner and Haight sts. No report of loss of life.

Along Market st. from 5th toward Castro, the sidewalks are literally strewn with wreckage. In many places the sidewalks have collapsed, falling into the basements.

This is true on Market between 5th and 6th, between 6th and 7th, and between 7th and City Hall Square, on the west side.

There are probably not fifty chimneys standing in the city. This means that many more fires are to be expected, as fires are cracked everywhere.

A small portion of the front of the West Side Christian Church was shaken out.

St. Ignatius' Church was badly shaken but is intact. Great damage resulted at St. Ignatius college, a portion of the building being destroyed.

A building was burned at the end of California street, in the Richmond.

Concordia Club, Van Ness Ave., badly dismantled.

At the Cosmopolitan Hotel, Fifth and Mission sts., fire is believed to have killed a number of people. The building was totally destroyed.

St. Winifred's hospital, Sutter near Larkin, was injured, but is intact.

At 9:30 the following were at Mechanics' Pavilion. But few were dead, although the injuries of many were reported as fatal:

Mrs Jones, 509 Stevenson; M R D Wells, 314 Van Ness; Wm Castro, roy, 410 1-4 Natoma; Bernard Atchison; 139 3rd; Ernest Edner, 1143 Mission; Bert Kennedy, 771 Howard; Geo Sullivan, 313 G G ave; Geo Memworth, 334 4th; Philip Hyndes, 3 Eddy; Wm Gamman, 112 4th, D J Erchon, 17 7th; Geo Rengone,

Glossary

corruption   wrongdoing that's against the law

....

graft   earning money in dishonest ways

....

immigrant   one who comes from another country

....

54

nicker   to whinny or neigh

proclamation official announcement

refugee   having to do with people who have left their homes

reliable   dependable

Richter Scale measurement that tells how much energy is in an earthquake. A reading of 1.5 indicates the smallest earthquake that can be felt. A 4.5 reading indicates a quake with slight damage. A 8.5 reading indicates a quake with severe damage. This scale was invented by Dr. Charles Richter.

sterilize	to make free of germs
tenor	highest adult male singing voice
tremor	movement following a major earthquake
wince	to draw back in pain